ISBN 0-8114-9305-9

7 8 9 0 1

Produced by Mega-Books of New York, Inc.
Design and Art Direction by Michaelis/Carpelis Design Assoc.

Cover illustration: Don Morrison

A BONE
TO PICK

by Leslie McGuire

interior illustrations by
Larry Raymond

STECK-VAUGHN
C O M P A N Y

Chapter One

"Wouldn't it be totally cool if we found some kind of treasure buried in this old wall?" Phoebe wondered out loud.

Adam, Carlos, and Phoebe were painting a mural on the outside wall of an old building. They had decided to brighten up the vacant lot next to Adam's building. They had already cleared the lot of trash. Then they had decided the wall of the building at the far side of the lot was a great spot for a painting. The three wanted to plant a garden, too.

"It would be even cooler if we found a million dollars," said Carlos.

"Why in the world would a million dollars be buried in this wall?" Adam asked Carlos.

"I don't know," Carlos answered. "Maybe some weird, rich person who was scared of banks hid lots of money here," he suggested.

"Dream on," said Adam laughing.

"If we found a million dollars, we could really fix up this lot with trees and benches," said Phoebe.

"And that old guy over there would sit on them, right?" said Adam. He nodded toward a gray-haired man standing nearby. The man was staring at them.

Phoebe looked over. "I bet he likes our painting," she said.

As Phoebe spoke, the man turned and slowly walked away. He looked over his shoulder once. Phoebe waved, but the man just bent his head and continued on his way.

Phoebe looked at the others and shrugged her shoulders.

"It looks more like he doesn't like our mural at all," said Adam.

"Hey!" Carlos cried. He had stopped painting. "There's a great big bump in this wall."

Phoebe went over to look. "It's going to ruin our painting," she groaned.

"How come we didn't notice this bump before?" Adam asked the others.

"I don't know," answered Phoebe. "But now we'll have to change the

7

picture. The bump is right in the middle."

The mural was going to be a picture of the neighborhood. In the background was the skyline and the bridge. Lower down would be the supermarket, drug store, bike shop, video store, pizza place, shoemaker, and some other stores. There would also be people hanging out and walking on the sidewalks. The bump was right on the edge of the place where a couple would be pushing a baby carriage. It would look pretty bad.

"We could move the people with the baby carriage and put a bush there," suggested Adam. "A bush wouldn't look too bad if it was bumpy."

"No," said Phoebe. "Bushes don't grow in the middle of the sidewalk!"

Carlos had an idea. "Don't worry," he said. "I can fix this easy!" He picked up a long piece of wood and started hitting the bump.

"I'll just flatten it," Carlos explained. He pounded the bump as hard as he could.

"Hey!" yelled Adam.

"Look out!" screamed Phoebe.

But before Carlos could move, a section of the wall gave way. A shower of bricks tumbled down.

Chapter Two

"Ouch! That hurt!" cried Carlos. He rubbed his shoulder.

But no one was looking at Carlos. Phoebe's mouth was hanging open in horror. Adam looked as if he was about to throw up. They were both staring at a hole in the wall.

"Hey, what's the matter with you?" Carlos said grouchily as he got up from the ground. "I just got hit with a pile of bricks, and you two just stand there!" Then Carlos's eyes followed Phoebe's and Adam's to the wall.

A skeleton stared back at them. It was propped up inside the hole. Its mouth hung open in a weird smile. Its empty

eye sockets looked angry.

Carlos gasped. Adam spit on the ground to calm his sick stomach. Phoebe put her hand over her mouth and moaned, "I think I'm going to lose my lunch."

"What should we do?" asked Carlos after a few moments. "We can't just leave this thing standing here." He turned to the others.

Phoebe stared at the skeleton and then at the boys. "Should we call the police?" she wondered out loud.

"Let's put the bricks back first," urged Adam. "That way we won't have to look at the skeleton while we decide what to do."

"Yeah," agreed Phoebe. "It's been here a long time. It can wait another day or two."

"I hope nobody else saw this thing," said Carlos as he looked around.

Phoebe, Adam, and Carlos quickly filled the hole with bricks before anyone came by. Then they decided to go to Adam's home to figure out what they should do.

"I think we have to tell the police," said Phoebe.

Carlos shook his head. "I'm not sure.

We might get in trouble for breaking the wall," he pointed out.

An hour later, they were still discussing their problem. Should they dig up the skeleton? Should they go to the police? Would they get in trouble? What would happen to their lot?

"Hey, why don't we try to dig up some clues to help the police first?," Phoebe suggested.

"How?" asked Adam and Carlos.

"Well," said Phoebe, thinking out loud. "Lots of people have lived around here for a long time. Maybe we can ask them about the history of the building."

A few hours later, Carlos, Phoebe, and Adam met again at Adam's home.

"This must have been a pretty wild neighborhood in the old days!" exclaimed Carlos.

"Tell me about it!" agreed Adam. "Mr. Torkin from the shoe store said there was an illegal gambling parlor behind his store."

"And Mrs. Ember from the flower shop said there were fancy nightclubs on Fourth Street," said Carlos. "In the 1920s, when drinking was against the law, they served liquor in coffee cups."

"So there were nightclubs, drinking, and gambling," said Phoebe. "But none of that helps us."

"So let's go search the building," said Adam. "Maybe we'll find some clues."

But when Adam, Carlos, and Phoebe got to the building, they couldn't get inside. The building was locked and boarded up. Outside they found lots of junk—old bottles, rags, pots, and a rotting painting—but not one clue.

Adam and Phoebe sat down in the

weeds. They were hot, thirsty, and about to give up. Carlos wandered off by himself.

All of a sudden Carlos yelled, "Hey, come here!" He was standing behind a clump of vines at the edge of the building.

Carlos was pointing down at something near the ground. "Look at that stone," he said.

"Reilly Construction Company 1943," Adam read out loud.

"That must be the cornerstone. It tells when the building was built," exclaimed Phoebe. "I bet that's when the body got put in the wall, too!"

"Yeah, but how can we know for sure?" asked Carlos.

"Let's go to the library," said Adam. "They have old newspapers on the computers."

"How will that help us?" Phoebe wanted to know.

"The papers may have stories about any trouble around here in 1943," explained Adam.

"Awesome idea!" said Carlos as he, Adam, and Phoebe slapped hands.

Chapter Three

Carlos was sitting at one of the computers in the library. "This is cool," he said as he scrolled through old newspaper pages on the screen in front of him.

"Yeah," Phoebe agreed. She was on a computer right next to Carlos. "They have every newspaper back to 1890!"

"Hey, listen to this," said Adam from his computer. " 'February 2, 1943. A Mrs. Lavilla Thomas reported her husband Martin, a bricklayer, missing. The police talked with the other bricklayers who worked for the Reilly Construction Company. They did not report anything odd about Mr. Thomas's behavior on the day he disappeared.' "

"Way to go!" yelled Carlos. The librarian frowned at him. Carlos leaned over and whispered to his friends, "Reilly Construction Company. I bet that's it!"

"Wait, there's more," Adam continued. "'Carl Reilly, the owner, said Mr. Thomas was his friend and a good worker. He had never missed a day on

the job until now. Foul play is suspected but cannot be proved.' "

"Cool," said Phoebe. "But how do we prove that the body in the wall is this Martin Thomas?"

"We have to see if there's anything lying near the skeleton that will tell us its name," said Adam. "We'll have to take down the bricks and look in that hole again."

"Yuck," said Carlos. "That's going to be disgusting!"

"And we'll have to go when it's dark, or people might see us," added Phoebe.

"Oh great," said Carlos, sounding nervous. "We're going to dig up a skeleton at night. This could be a real horror show."

By nine o'clock it was dark. Adam, Phoebe, and Carlos met on the corner, each carrying a flashlight. They began walking to the vacant lot.

"This is spooky," whispered Phoebe as they rounded the corner to the lot.

"Quiet!" ordered Adam, pointing.
"Look over there."

A shadowy figure was standing by the
wall. The figure seemed to be trying to
pull the bricks out of the wall—right at
the spot where they had found the
skeleton!

"Oh great!" groaned Carlos. "We have a visitor. Somebody else knows."

Just then the figure stopped and stared in their direction. Then the figure turned and hurried away into the night.

"Trail that person!" said Adam.

"Who? Me?" whispered Carlos.

"Stay a safe distance away," Adam told him. "Find out where the person goes so we can go back later. And stay out of sight. Don't let the person see you. We'll check the skeleton."

Carlos took off. Phoebe and Adam started pulling bricks from the wall. Phoebe gulped when she saw the skeleton's grin.

Phoebe shined her flashlight into the hole. Adam did the same. They beamed their lights around. Something caught the light.

"Hey, what's that shiny thing on the ground?" asked Adam.

"I'll get it," offered Phoebe.

Phoebe reached inside the hole. She shuddered as her arm brushed against the old bones. Then her fingers closed around something hard and round.

"It's a ring!" Phoebe cried as she held it in front of the light. "And there's writing inside," she added. "It says, 'With Love from LT 1940.' "

Just then Carlos came dashing across the lot. He was out of breath.

"It was an old guy," gasped Carlos. "He went into the apartment over the deli. The name on the apartment doorbell is Reilly!"

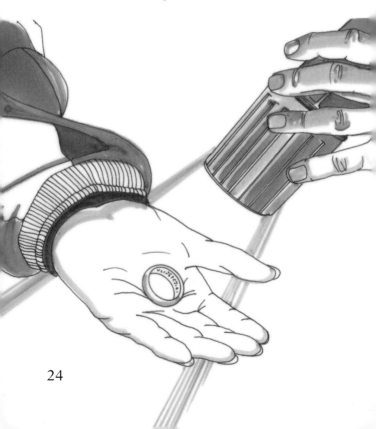

Chapter Four

"Reilly?" cried Adam. "You mean like in Reilly Construction Company?"

"I mean like in Carl Reilly. I'll bet he's the killer," cried Carlos. "And I bet he was looking for this ring. Let's go to the police."

"The ring isn't proof," said Phoebe.

"Why else would that old guy be pulling out the bricks?" Carlos asked.

"The police probably won't believe us anyway," said Phoebe. "But maybe the ring is some kind of clue."

Phoebe looked at the ring carefully. "Who is LT?" she wondered out loud.

"Didn't that old newspaper say the wife of the missing bricklayer was named Lavilla?" asked Carlos. "And their last name was Thomas. LT stands for Lavilla Thomas!"

"So the ring belongs to the skeleton. That means we still need proof that Carl Reilly is the murderer," said Adam.

"Let's stake out his apartment," suggested Phoebe.

An hour later, Phoebe, Adam, and Carlos were still hiding near the deli. Then suddenly the front door of the apartment building opened. Out stepped an old man.

"Far out!" whispered Adam. "Reilly's the old guy who was watching us paint our mural. He's got to be the murderer."

They rushed up to the old man.

"Leave me alone!" the man shouted. "Go away or I'll call the police!"

"That's exactly what we want you to do. We want you to tell them about Martin Thomas," said Carlos.

"And about this ring," added Phoebe.

The old man looked at the ring closely

and gasped. "That's Marty's wedding ring," he sighed. "I'm Carl Reilly. I was Marty's boss. I was also the best man at his wedding. And I know what you kids are thinking. But I swear it was an accident."

"What was an accident?" asked Phoebe.

"Marty and I were laying bricks on that building next to your vacant lot," Carl Reilly explained. "And I accidentally kicked a pile of bricks that were on the scaffold."

Reilly stopped speaking for a moment. He looked as if he was going to cry.

"One of the bricks hit Marty in the head," Reilly finally continued. "It killed him immediately."

"How come you put him behind the brick wall?" Phoebe wanted to know.

"I was scared," explained Reilly. "I know it was wrong, but I couldn't think of anything else to do at the time. When you kids found Marty's skeleton, I decided it was time to turn myself in."

They all went to the police station. After the questioning, Adam, Phoebe, and Carlos were thanked. Then they were told to leave.

The next morning Adam, Phoebe, and Carlos met at the vacant lot. The wall with their mural was blocked off with yellow tape. They couldn't get near it.

Adam was carrying a newspaper. "Hey look!" he said, all excited. "We're famous. The story is in the paper. And they talk about us!"

Carlos took the newspaper from Adam. He began to read the story out loud.

"The paper says Carl Reilly is not being charged with murder," Carlos read. "They say it was involuntary manslaughter."

Phoebe frowned. "Great, but when can we finish painting our mural?" she asked sadly.

"The police have to finish their work there, first," said Carlos.

"We can start working on the garden instead," suggested Adam. "We can finish the mural when the police take down the tape."

"You know what?" said Phoebe. "I think we should paint something really special on the wall."

"What do you mean?" asked Carlos.

"We could paint a rainbow or something over the spot where Martin Thomas was buried all these years,"

Phoebe explained. "The wall could be a sort of memorial to him."

Adam smiled at his friends. "We're going to make this mural the best thing in our neighborhood," he exclaimed proudly.

"And we solved a really old mystery, too!" chimed in Carlos

"No bones about it!" Phoebe joked.